A Halloween Tale

Dawn Muir

Illustrated by Raymond Cramb

www.dawnmuir.co.uk

First published in Great Britain in 2020
by Raymond Cramb
Stirling, Scotland.

Published by Raymond Cramb 2020

Have a spooky Halloween!

It is Halloween tonight

and the full moon is big and bright.

It's not safe to go out guising this year,

because the whole world is living in fear!

You see there is something out there that we cannot see.

So, I'm not chancing it, no not me!

Instead, I'm choosing the safety of hame.

I hope you all do the same.

So, let's tell stories from old folklore.

That will scare you, forevermore!

You see, in the still of the night.

The Brollachan creeps just out of sight!

Through the Abbey graveyard,
where seven kings lie.

Past the clock tower, way up high.

Andrew Carnegie looks down from above.

Watching over his birthplace, his first love.

The witches hat looms in the night.

As ravens caw and take flight.

Above a scurry of squirrels jump through the trees.

While the peacocks stroll below, quite at their ease.

It only comes out on this one special night.

After that, it will disappear back out of sight.

It rattles at the windows and bangs on the door.

The grown ups don't hear it, they tell us "Wheesht, say no more!"

There's a chapping at the letterbox,
something posted through the door.

Lots of sweets and chocolate
landing on the floor.

Something is trying to entice us outside!

We aren't crazy, come on everyone hide!

As long as we stay inside until Dawn.

Then, for sure it will be gone!

For another nineteen years it will sleep.

Until it wakes once more and out it will creep!

Printed in Great Britain
by Amazon